If You Take a Pencil

Dial Books for Young Readers
A Division of E. P. Dutton, Inc.
2 Park Avenue
New York, New York 10016

Library of Congress Catalog Card Number: 82-1505
Printed in Italy
First Pied Piper Printing 1985
A Pied Piper Book is a registered trademark of
Dial Books for Young Readers,
a division of E. P. Dutton, Inc.,
®TM 1,163,686 and ®TM 1,054,312

IF YOU TAKE A PENCIL
is published in a hardcover edition by
Dial Books for Young Readers.
ISBN 0-8037-0165-9

The art for each picture consists of an ink
and dye painting, which is camera-separated
and reproduced in full color.

If You Take a Pencil

FULVIO TESTA

Dial Books for Young Readers

E. P. DUTTON, INC.   *New York*

If you take a pencil, you can draw two cats.

And if they like each other, there will soon be three.

They will flirt with four birds in a golden cage.

And five fingers can give them freedom.

They will fly into a garden with six orange trees.

Nearby is a fountain with seven jets of fresh water.

In the fountain are eight red fish with blue tails—

blue like the sea where there is a boat with nine sails.

Ten are the sailors.

Eleven are the small islands around the treasure island.

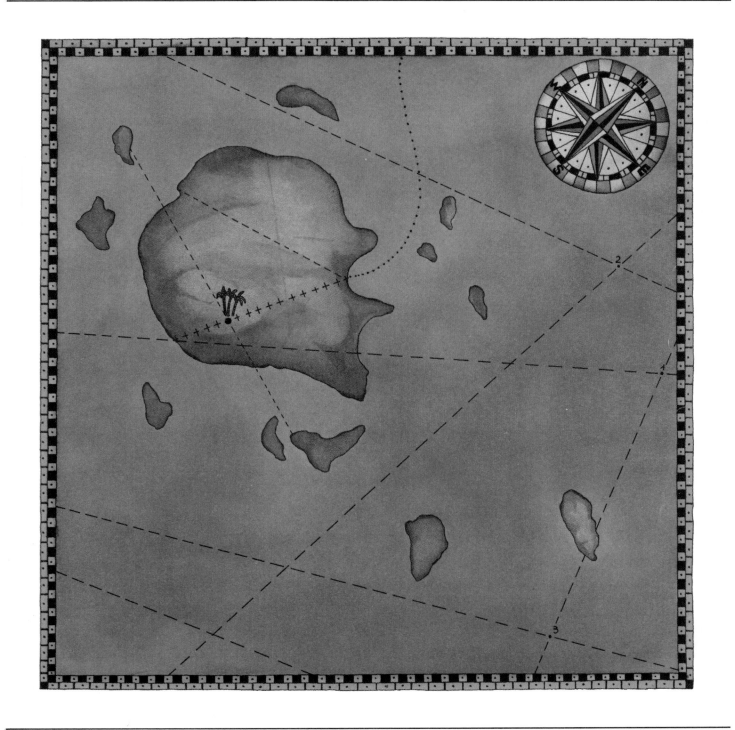

On the island are twelve treasure chests.
They are all empty except one.

You open it. There is a little treasure inside—
a pencil.

Fulvio Testa

"The artist's style, combining lessons with entertainment, is beguiling," raved *Publishers Weekly* about Fulvio Testa's work. And *The Horn Book* added, "With something of the visual ingenuity and playfulness of Mitsumasa Anno but with his own precise style, the Italian artist...piques interest, stimulates imagination, and encourages observation and discussion."

Fulvio Testa was trained in Italy as an architect. He is the author-illustrator of more than a dozen books, which have been published in the United States, Europe, and Japan. Among his recent titles are *If You Take a Pencil, If You Take a Paintbrush: A Book of Colors, If You Look Around You,* and *If You Seek Adventure* (all Dial).

Fulvio Testa is a painter and sculptor as well as an illustrator. He lives in New York City.

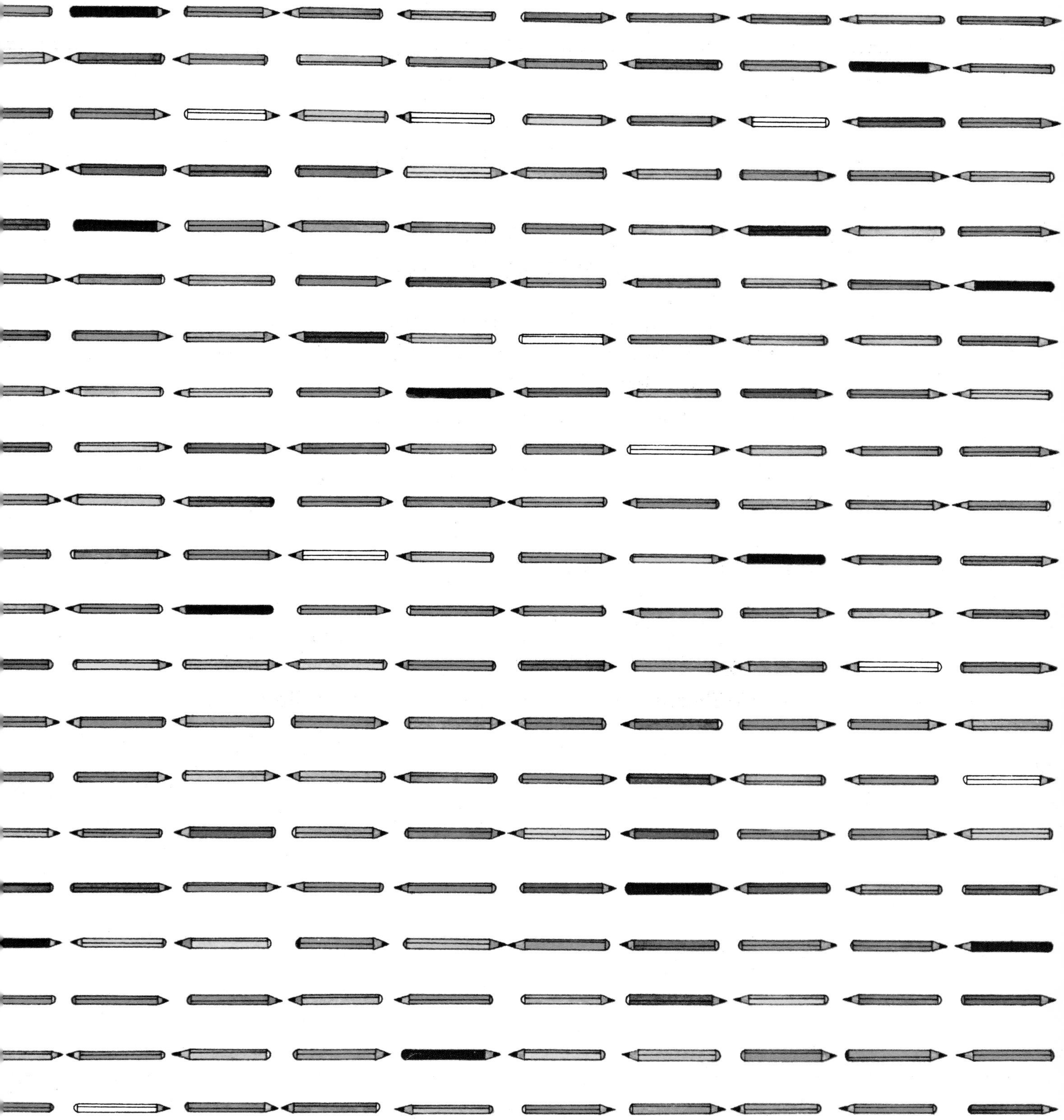

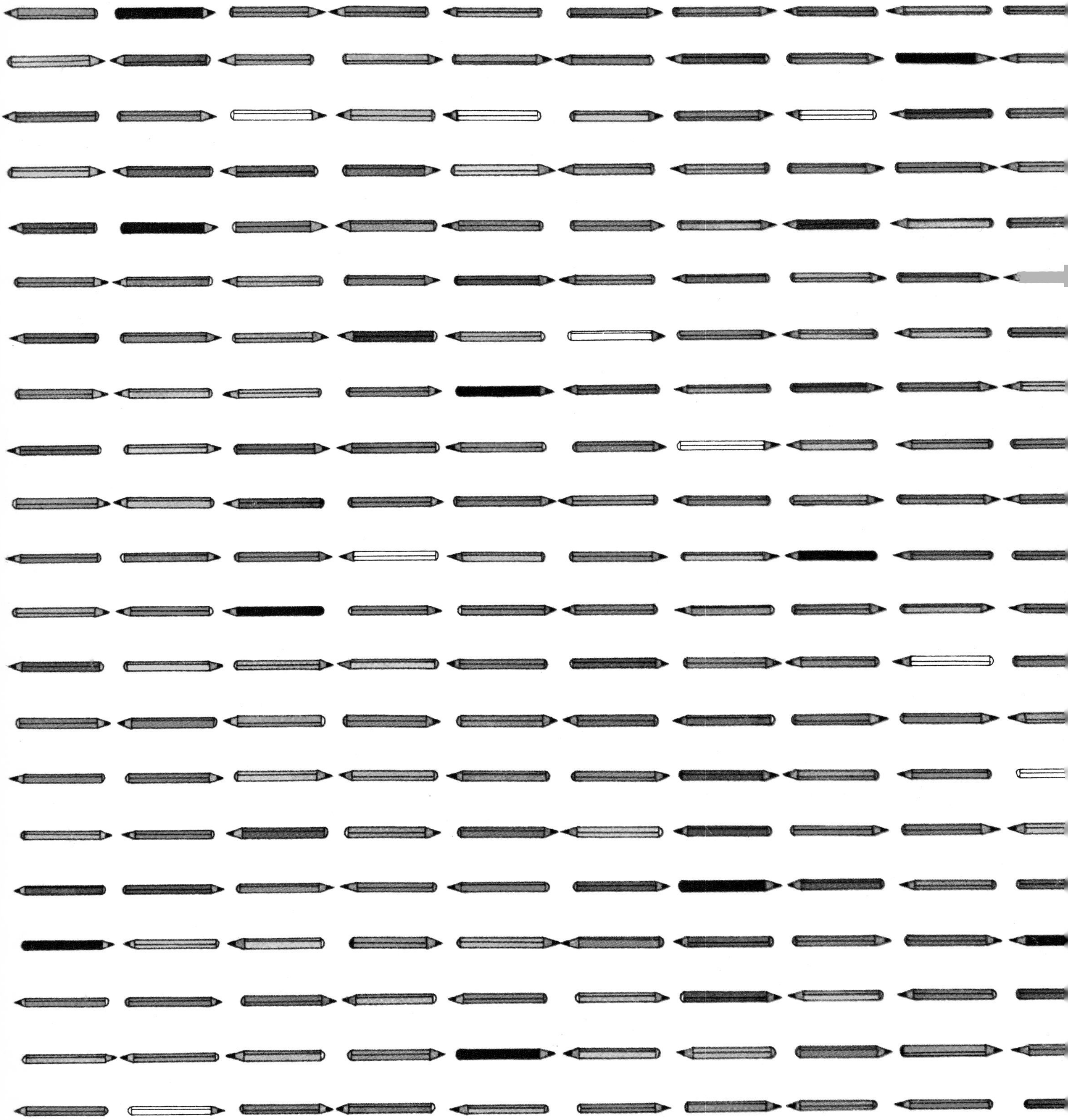